Flo & Wendell (SOMETIMES)

William Wegman

 Dial Books for Young Readers
an imprint of Penguin Group (USA) Inc.

for Atlas & Lola

DIAL BOOKS FOR YOUNG READERS

A division of Penguin Young Readers Group • Published by the Penguin Group

Penguin Group (USA) Inc., 375 Hudson Street, New York, New York 10014, USA

USA | Canada | UK | Ireland | Australia | New Zealand | India | South Africa | China

Penguin Books Ltd, Registered Offices: 80 Strand, London WC2R 0RL, England

For more information about the Penguin Group visit penguin.com

The artwork for this book was created with gouache on photographs.

With special thanks to: Jason Burch, Emily Helck and Christine Burgin,
Jake Wotherspoon, Gene and Renée LaFollette, Brian and Beth Meany,
Nancy Conescu and Lily Malcom, Ken Swezey, Dorian Karchmar.

This is Flo.

What's your name?

Is it Flo, too?

Flo is very sophisticated.

She can read and write.

She can even tie her shoes.

When she was little she couldn't.

She didn't have shoes.

Flo's father is an artist.

He likes to paint.

Flo is an artist, too.

She likes paint.

Flo's mother is wild about knitting.

She knit a sweater for Flo
and one for their car.

Now Flo and their car match.

This is Flo's little brother, Wendell.

He likes to play hide-and-seek.

Wendell hides. Flo seeks . . .

. . . sometimes.

Sometimes Flo doesn't bother.

Too much bother looking for brother.

Once Wendell hid in a can and got stuck.

HELP

Flo took her time getting him out.

Flo's parents say she is very dramatic.

She does like to dress up.

Wendell does, too . . .

. . . sometimes.

Sometimes Wendell has other ideas.

Flo and Wendell's parents wish they would
find something to do together.

Maybe badminton?

What about a lemonade stand?

Or cooking? Flo and Wendell both like to cook.

Flo measures all her ingredients precisely.

Wendell is more experimental.

Anything goes.

Flo's cupcakes come out perfectly.

Some of Wendell's recipes are better than others.

But no matter what, at the end of each day,
Flo likes to read

and Wendell likes to listen.

Sometimes.

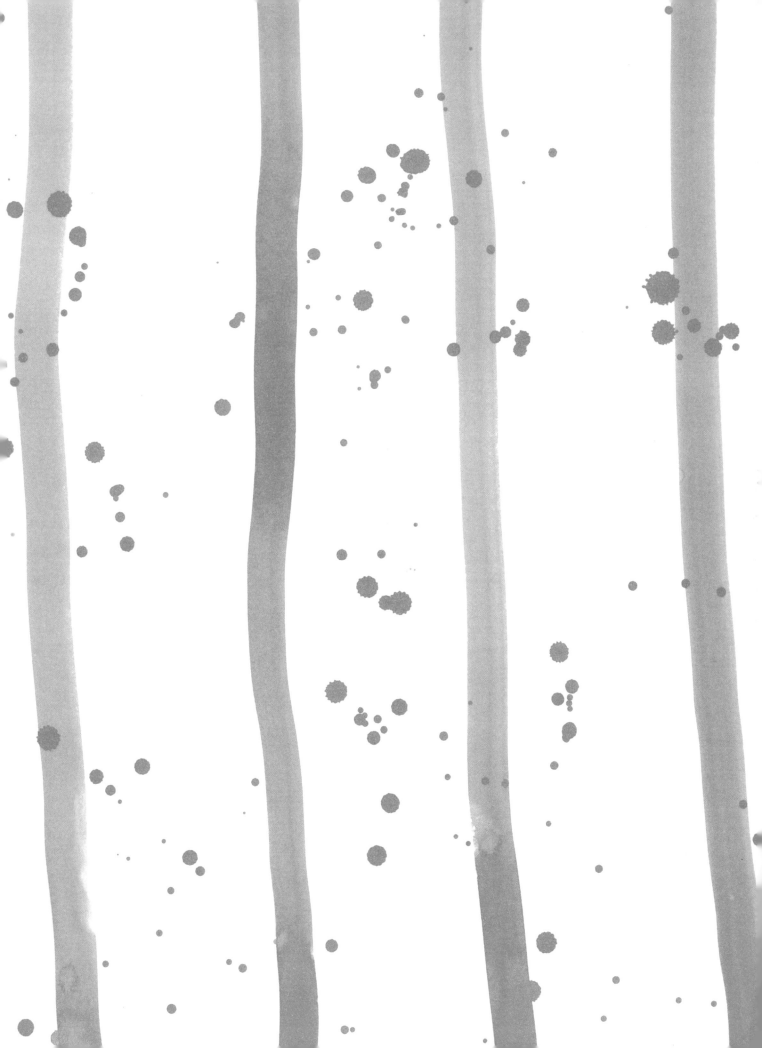